Cinderella's Dress

by NANCY WILLARD

illustrated by JANE DYER

SCHOLASTIC INC.

New York Toronto London Auckland Sydney
Mexico City New Delhi Hong Kong Buenos Aires

The black magpie is very rare

and only seen by those who share

the power to make a wish come true.

I pass the secret on to you.

12 11 10 9 8 7 6 5 4 3   5 6 7 8 9/0
Printed in the U.S.A.   08
First Scholastic paperback printing, May 2004
Special thanks to my daughter Brooke
for helping me imagine this book. - J.D.
Handlettering by David Coulson

FOR TINA AND PAUL KANE

N. W.

FOR MARIA MODUGNO,

who knows a good dress when she sees one

J. D.

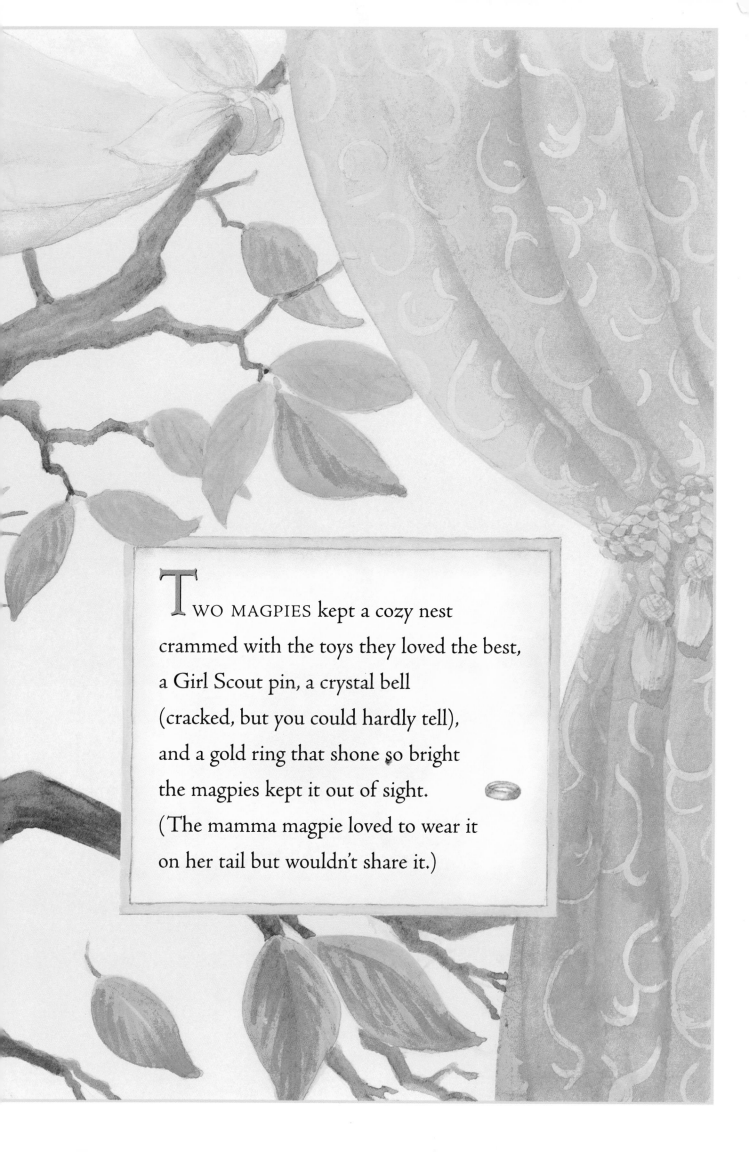

Two magpies kept a cozy nest
crammed with the toys they loved the best,
a Girl Scout pin, a crystal bell
(cracked, but you could hardly tell),
and a gold ring that shone so bright
the magpies kept it out of sight.
(The mamma magpie loved to wear it
on her tail but wouldn't share it.)

Their specialty was shiny paper,
foil and tissue, squares of lace,
from which they clipped,
folded, and snipped
a golden wreath, a silver shoe
half bright, half blue,
an emerald fan, a leopard's face
with snowflakes dangling from its ear,
a clipper ship as light as foam.
You should have seen their scissors caper.

Their nest allowed the pair to peer
into a wealthy merchant's home.
His new wife nagged him day and night.
Her daughters had the whole upstairs.
They fought and yanked each other's hair;
they broke a watch, the bathroom light.
They threw away a mended shawl.
The thrifty magpies saved it all.

The tree in which they kept their store
stood close behind the kitchen door,
not far from where they'd found the ring.
The girl who scrubbed the pots and pans
wore nothing bright on her rough hands.
She scoured the house from roof to cellar,
and slept in soot. "How well she sings!"
the magpie mamma told her mate.
"Her sisters call her Cinderella.
Her hair is black as magpies' wings.
She lights the stove and draws the water.
Her father's weak, her mother's dead.
Nobody tucks her into bed.
This stepsister they love to hate,
let's make her our adopted daughter—"

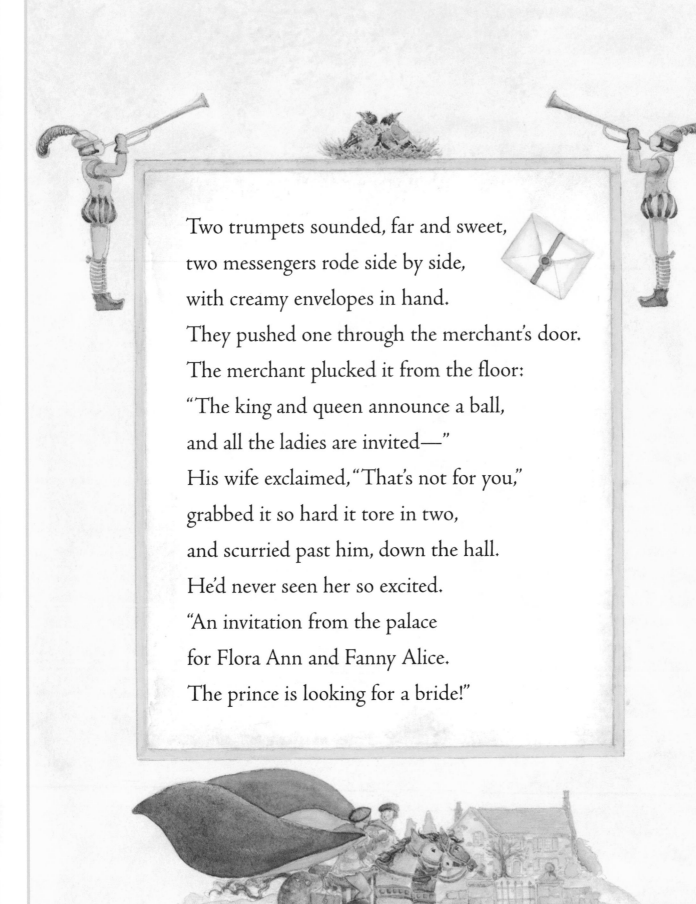

Two trumpets sounded, far and sweet,
two messengers rode side by side,
with creamy envelopes in hand.
They pushed one through the merchant's door.
The merchant plucked it from the floor:
"The king and queen announce a ball,
and all the ladies are invited—"
His wife exclaimed, "That's not for you,"
grabbed it so hard it tore in two,
and scurried past him, down the hall.
He'd never seen her so excited.
"An invitation from the palace
for Flora Ann and Fanny Alice.
The prince is looking for a bride!"

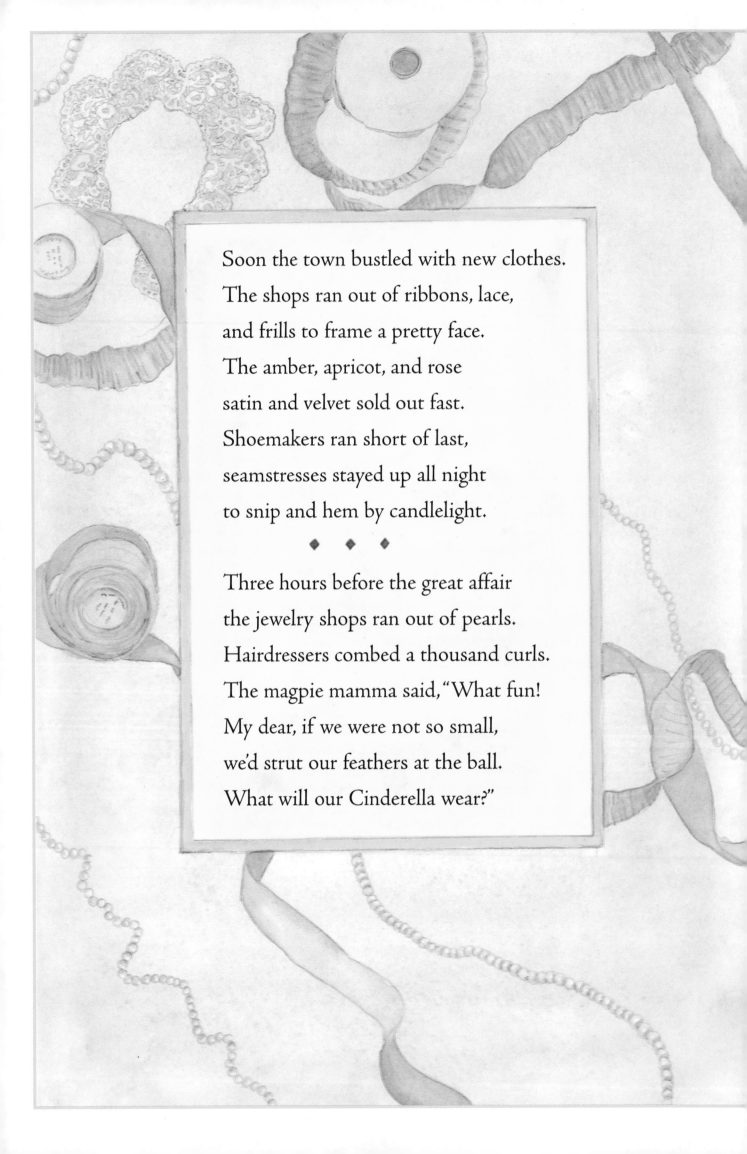

Soon the town bustled with new clothes.
The shops ran out of ribbons, lace,
and frills to frame a pretty face.
The amber, apricot, and rose
satin and velvet sold out fast.
Shoemakers ran short of last,
seamstresses stayed up all night
to snip and hem by candlelight.

◆　◆　◆

Three hours before the great affair
the jewelry shops ran out of pearls.
Hairdressers combed a thousand curls.
The magpie mamma said, "What fun!
My dear, if we were not so small,
we'd strut our feathers at the ball.
What will our Cinderella wear?"

Just then the shutters opened wide.
The birds kept still and peeped inside.

"Cinderella, curl my hair."
"Cinderella, don't you dare
do Flora's hair before I'm done."
"Mend my gown." "Clean my shoe
before I kick you black and blue."
"Our carriage comes at half past eight.
Let's go downstairs, Fanny, and wait."

The magpie mamma cocked her head,
admired her glossy wings, and said,
"Let's make a dress as bright as water
to fit our featherless young daughter,
if we can finish it in time.
No shop in town equals our nest
for things that shimmer, dream, and shine."
They glued and gathered, poked and pinched
rose-petal tissue, silver thread.
They pleated petticoats. They cinched
the tiny waist with amethysts.

◆　　◆　　◆

They trimmed the sleeves
with golden leaves
clipped from the wreath they took apart.
An emerald fan to cool her wrist,
a topaz cat to hold her hair,
a ruby purse with silver handles,
and strapless, backless silver sandals.
The magpie papa coughed and said,
"My clever wife, my honey dear,
that golden ring you hate to share
would gladden any young girl's heart."
The magpie mamma shook her head.
"Oh, she has lots of things that shine,
her fan, her sleeves. The ring is mine."

They viewed their handiwork with pride
and hung it on the kitchen door. . . .

When Cinderella stepped inside,
meaning to scrub the kitchen floor,
she dropped the scrub bucket and broom,
took a deep breath and rubbed her eyes.
"The dress I've dreamed of—just my size!
Whoever sent me this," she cried,
"a hundred thanks, a thousand more."
It seemed to light the very room.
Light gleamed on every pot and plate,
polished the apples, plums, and pears.
She put it on, and every fold
fitted, and gathered her in gold.
The kitchen clock chimed half past eight.
She rode the bannister downstairs
so fast she nearly lost a shoe.
"Dear sisters, wait,
I'm coming, too!"

Nobody saw two magpies fly
through open shutters, seat themselves
like bookends on the highest shelves,
and watch the sisters stare and glower,
at Cinderella skipping by.
"You little thief, you stole that dress,"
hissed Fanny. Flora Ann made faces
as if she'd eaten something sour.
"Your petticoat's a real mess.
I'll fix it, sister dear," she grinned
and yanked the skirt, which came unpinned
and tore in half a dozen places.
"Why, this is paper!" she exclaimed.
"A dress so cheap, a price so petty,
it's good for nothing but confetti."
A tug, a rip, a tear, a clatter
of cocoa cups that spill and spatter.
Fanny let out a joyful yelp.
"You can't wear something torn and stained."
She held up half a tattered sleeve.
"So sorry, dear. We tried to help.
Mother is calling. Time to leave."